MY NIGHT FOREST

MY NIGHT FOREST

by Roy Owen

illustrated by Amy Córdova

Four Winds Press   New York
Maxwell Macmillan Canada   Toronto
Maxwell Macmillan International
New York   Oxford   Singapore   Sydney

Four Winds Press
Macmillan Publishing Company
866 Third Avenue
New York, NY 10022

Maxwell Macmillan Canada, Inc.
1200 Eglinton Avenue East
Suite 200
Don Mills, Ontario M3C 3N1

Macmillan Publishing Company is part of the
Maxwell Communication Group of Companies.

First edition
Printed in Singapore on recycled paper
10 9 8 7 6 5 4 3 2 1

The text of this book is set in Garamond.
The illustrations are rendered in mixed media.
Book design by Christy Hale

Library of Congress Cataloging-in-Publication Data
Owen, Roy. My night forest / by Roy Owen ;
illustrated by Amy Córdova. — 1st ed.
p.   cm.
Summary: A child tries to imagine what an owl sees,
what a wolf hears, what a bear smells, what a deer tastes,
and what a mouse touches.
ISBN 0-02-769005-9
[1. Senses and sensation—Fiction.   2. Imagination—Fiction.
3. Animals—Fiction.]   I. Córdova, Amy, ill.   II. Title.
PZ7.O9715My   1994
[E]—dc20   93-45666

I f I could see what the owl sees,
I think I could see where the young salmon go.

I think I could see where the dew comes from
and where in the nighttime the mouse hides her babies
and where rivers rise
and where new moons set
and how many grass blades there are in the meadow
and how many pebbles there are on the beach,

if I could see what the owl sees.

If I could hear what the wolf hears,
I think I could hear the owl on the wing.

I think I could hear what the mouse tells her babies
and where the deer goes as it moves through the forest
and how many waves wash onto the shore
and how many salmon lie in the deep pools
and when a twig falls far in the forest
and the breath of a cricket
and the sigh of a bear,

if I could hear what the wolf hears.

If I could smell what the bear smells,
I think I could smell what tomorrow might bring.

I think I could smell yesterday's footfalls
and how many salmon lie in the deep pools
and where the owl flies in the dark of the moon
and where the mouse sleeps
and where the wolf waits
and where berries bloom
and what's in the quiet of the gathering darkness,

if I could smell what the bear smells.

I f I could taste what the deer tastes,
I think I could taste the dew on the breeze.

I think I could taste the ripening berries
in the swift-flowing waters of a cold, rushing stream
and the promise of springtime in the bud of an aspen
and the depth of the earth in the tender young grasses
and where in the forest the lichen grows thickest
and what's in the fog
and where the wolf waits,

if I could taste what the deer tastes.

If I could touch what the mouse touches,
I think I could touch the curve of a dewdrop.

I think I could feel the warmth of the earth
and the cool of an iris
and the breath of an aspen
and the steps of the wolf as it walks through the forest
and all of the babies who have slept here before me,

if I could touch what the mouse touches.

Come now, my sweet one, it's time now for bed.
The darkness has gathered, the world has grown still.

The mouse in the nighttime is hiding her babies.

The wolf in the forest is listening quietly.

The owl's on the wing.

The bear's in his den.

The deer are safe where it is deer go.

Maybe tomorrow we can walk in the forest
and follow the river down to the beach
and search for the owl
and listen for the wolf
and watch for the deer
and watch for the bear
and find in the meadow the path of the mouse and
follow the path to the mouse and her babies.